Summer Moonlight Concert

Story and Illustrations Han Han

It was a summer evening. A gentle, steady breeze blew as the setting sun reflected from a distance. Light appeared red on the horizon.

Parents walked home holding their children's hand. They headed towards the apartment building with bags of vegetables as, one by one, the lights went on in each dwelling.

Xiaomi's apartment was on the fourth floor where her family was busy preparing dinner. Dad washed the rice while she helped her Mom sort the vegetables. The food cooking in the kitchen smelled so good.

The moon was out while the stars twinkled in the sky.

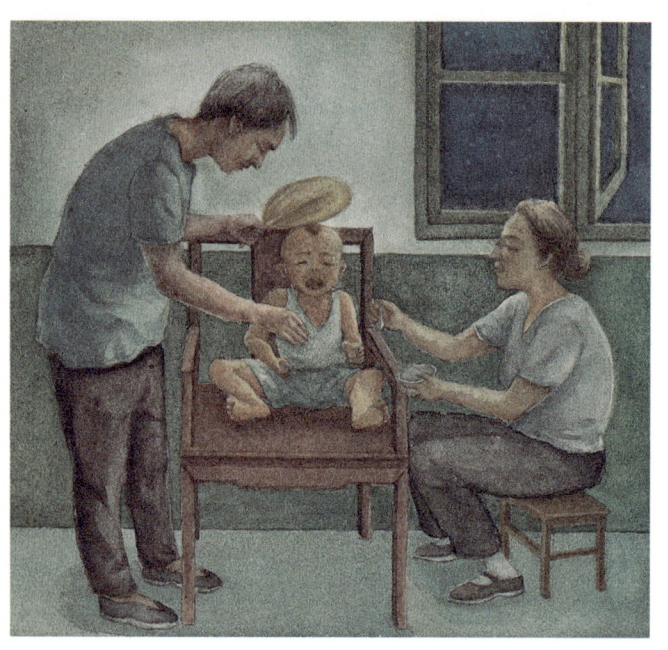

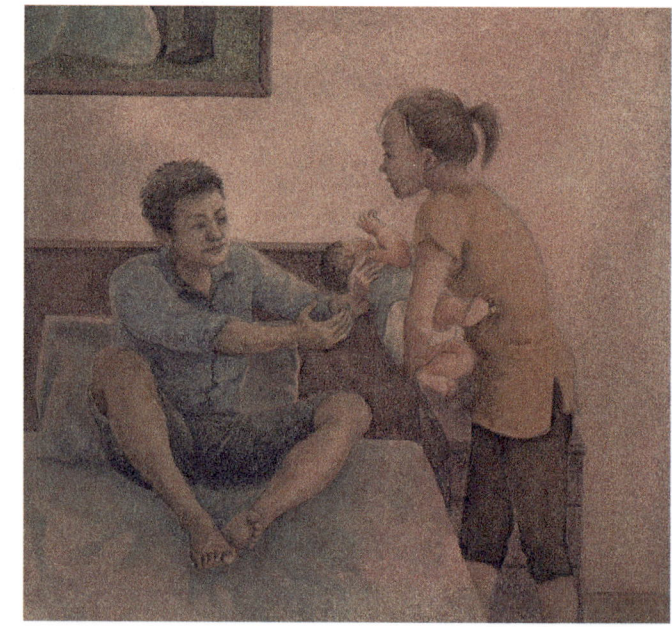

The family had just finished eating dinner.

"I haven't done my homework yet," complained Xiaomi.

"And the dishes haven't been done either," Mom added.

"Don't worry," Dad replied as he lit candles by the window, "look at that stunning moonlight, we should do a concert outside in the yard."

"We really should!" exclaimed Xiaomi, thrilled with the idea.

Dad took out the erhu, mom the accordion.

Xiaomi held a flashlight and went ahead of them down the stairs.

The silver moon flickered cheerfully over the yard.

Dad sat down near the flower bed with the erhu and began playing in the key of G.

Do-re-me-fa...

He then changed key, creating a swirling melody. Mom was beaming as she followed along with the accordion.

Xiaomi danced while she introduced the musicians. "The first song is called *The Moonlight Evening*"

It was truly magical. Not a sound could be heard coming from the building now that the neighbors had gathered in the yard.

The babies had stopped crying; the children weren't running around, and the parents watched the musicians, thoroughly enjoying the performance.

Dad turned to mom leaning towards her ear, "Let's play a catchy song that will make our neighbors dance."

The moon smiled upon them
as they danced and laughed.

As Dad played the last note, he announced that the concert was over.

Xiaomi joined in, "See you next time, you are always welcome!"

Everyone clapped and thanked the musicians for an unforgettable summer moonlight concert. As they returned home, the music continued to dance in their hearts.

Story and illustrations Han Han
Theme Song Liu Tianhua (*Beautiful Evening* / 良宵)
Narration Anie Richer
Recording producer and musical arrangement Jean François Groulx
Musicians Jean-François Groulx (percussions, keyboards)
Patty Chan (erhu) and Lucio Altobelli (accordion)
Design Stephan Lorti for Haus Design
Translation Xinyi Tan
Copy editor Ruth Joseph for Tangerine Media

First published in Chinese as *The Summer Evening Concert* (夏夜音乐会) ©2015 Han Han / 含含 (text and illustrations), ©2015 Beijing POPLAR Culture Project Co., Ltd. English translation rights arranged with Beijing POPLAR Culture Project Co., Ltd.

The picture book is accompanied by a 8-minute CD of the narrated story and the theme song. A unique code for the digital download of the recordings and a printable file of the illustrated story is included with this book-CD.

www.thesecretmountain.com
2021 The Secret Mountain (Folle Avoine Productions)
ISBN 13: 978-2-924774-87-8 / ISBN 10: 2-924774-87-X

All rights reserved. No part of this publication may be reproduced or transmitted in any form or by any means, electronic or mechanical, including photocopying, recording or any information storage and retrieval system, without permission in writing from the publisher. Printed in China.